FURRY AND FLO

capstone
young readers

Furry and Flo is published by
Capstone Young Readers
A Capstone Imprint
1710 Roe Crest Drive
North Mankato, MN 56003
www.capstoneyoungreaders.com

Library of Congress Cataloging-in-Publication Data is available on the Library of Congress website.

Summary: Furry and Flo find themselves in an ancient land chasing after a misplaced mummy -- and some very important belongings!

  ISBN 978-1-4342-6396-4 (library binding) -- ISBN 978-1-62370-047-8 (paper over board) -- ISBN 978-1-4342-9244-5 (eBook PDF)

Artistic effects: Shutterstock/Kataleks Studio (background)

Book design by Hilary Wacholz.

Printed in China.
092013   007733LEOS14

THE MISPLACED MUMMY

BOOK 3

BY THOMAS KINGSLEY TROUPE
ILLUSTRATED BY STEPHEN GILPIN

TABLE OF

CONTENTS

SAND!

CHAPTER 1

"Florence Gardner! Get out here this instant!"

Flo sighed with annoyance. Her mother knew how much she hated to be called Florence. She tossed aside the comic book she was reading, rolled off her bed, and headed into the living room of their small apartment.

Flo's mom stood near the worn recliner they'd dragged with them from house to house and finally into their apartment at

Corman Towers, a high-rise building in the middle of the city. Like Flo, the chair couldn't handle another move.

"Really, Mom? *Florence?*" Flo asked, putting her hands on her hips.

"Have you been to the park lately?" Flo's mom asked, as if she hadn't just called her *that* name.

Flo shrugged. "Yeah," she said. "School starts next week, so Furry and I are there practically every day. Summer's almost over, Mom. We have to take advantage of the last few days."

Her mom motioned to the front door. "Do you need to bring the park back with you?" she asked. "The hallway is covered in sand."

"What do you mean?" Flo asked. She walked across the outdated carpet and tugged the door open. She figured her mom was exaggerating but wanted to see for herself.

But when Flo stuck her head out into the hallway, she realized her mom was right. It looked like someone had dumped an entire sandbox out and raked it across the carpet.

"I didn't do that," Flo protested. "I wouldn't even know *how* to do that."

Mom threw her hands up. "You and Furry are the only kids on this floor," she said. "The neighbors are sure it's the two of you. The doctor down the hall seems to think you and Furry are trouble."

He wouldn't think that if he knew all the trouble we've stopped, Flo thought.

Since she and her mom had moved into Corman Towers a few months ago, Flo had discovered that their new home was *far* from normal. For starters, Furry wasn't just a regular kid. He was a werewolf. And then there was the creepy crack in the basement laundry room. As Flo had learned, it was more than just a crack — it was a portal to another world. A world full of monsters.

So far, Furry and Flo had managed to defend the building against the giant spiders and goblins that had slipped through the crack. But they hadn't been able to close it up for good. Which meant more monsters could come through at any time.

As much as Flo wanted to, she knew she couldn't tell her mom about Furry's secret or any of the creepy things that had come out of the mysterious crack in the basement.

"I'll talk to Furry," Flo said. "But c'mon, Mom. Don't blame the kids every time something goes wrong."

Her mom got up and headed to the kitchen to start dinner, and Flo grabbed her trusty Dyno-Katz lunchbox off the floor. "I'm going to see Furry," she called as she opened the front door and walked out into the sandy hallway. The gritty sand immediately crunched beneath her shoes.

That's so weird, Flo thought. *Where did all this sand come from?*

Flo walked down the hallway to Furry's apartment and knocked on the front door. It swung open almost immediately, and Furry stood there, wearing a pair of worn-looking swim trunks.

Flo rolled her eyes. Furry never seemed to be wearing clothes. At first she'd thought it was weird, but now she knew it had more to do with Furry being a werewolf than anything else.

Not that it isn't still weird, Flo thought. Just then, she noticed a thin piece of blue stone tied to a cord around Furry's neck. It looked sort of like a faded piece of blue chalk. But it was skinnier and rougher looking. She'd never seen him wear it before.

"What's with the necklace?" Flo asked. For a moment she forgot all about the sand problem.

"Oh, this?" Furry asked. He put his fingers around it, as if to protect it. "It's sort of a family heirloom."

"Did you get it from your parents?" Flo asked. "Your real ones, I mean."

Furry looked at the ground and avoided her gaze. "Yeah, I guess you could say that," he said.

"What is it?" Flo asked. Now she was really curious.

"Something from my world," Furry said. "I'll tell you about it later. Right now, we've got trouble."

Flo sighed. "Again?" she asked.

"Again," Furry replied.

"What is it this time?" Flo asked.

"There's a mummy wandering around the hallway," Furry announced.

Flo's mouth dropped open, and she stared at her friend in shock. "What?" she cried. "You mean like a dead guy wrapped up in toilet paper? That kind of mummy?"

Furry laughed. "Toilet paper?" he repeated. "That's hilarious."

"How are you being so calm about this?" Flo exclaimed. "How did it get here? Did it come through the crack in the basement?"

Furry shrugged. "Probably."

"I thought we covered it really well last time!" Flo said. "What are we still doing up here? Let's go!"

"Okay, okay," Furry said. "Jeez. Let's go find ourselves a mummy."

A DUMMY MUMMY

CHAPTER 2

Furry and Flo followed the incriminating trail of sand all the way down the long hallway.

"So does the mummy have anything to do with all this sand?" Flo asked.

"Yeah," Furry replied. "Mummies live under the sand in my world. It gets stuck all over them. Most of the sand probably fell off while it was wandering around."

Flo shuddered. She didn't know how Furry slept at night, knowing what kind of creatures might be wandering around. *First the spider, then the goblins, and now a mummy?* she thought. *It's enough to give a girl nightmares.*

The sand grew thicker on the floor as they reached the door to the stairwell. "The goblins weren't enough?" Flo said. "Now a mummy wants to find you, too?"

Furry shrugged. "I don't know if it really wants to find me. Mummies aren't exactly the smartest monsters. He might have just fallen through on his own."

"How?" Flo asked. "Aren't mummies dead kings and queens? Like pharaohs? Shouldn't he be in a fancy tomb someplace?"

Furry shook his head. "Mummies from my world aren't like the ones in yours," he explained. "They're not important people. They just sort of . . . swim around in the sand. Maybe this one got lost or something."

The lightbulb was burnt out in the stairwell on their floor, making it hard to see where they were going. Furry got down on his hands and knees and sniffed the ground.

"This mummy really is a dummy," Furry said, shaking his head. "He was right in our

hallway, but it smells like he ended up going upstairs."

Flo shuddered. The idea of a mummy seriously freaked her out. Even more than the other creatures they'd faced. A mummy was basically a zombie wrapped up like a rotten birthday present. And there was one stumbling around Corman Towers? It made her skin crawl.

"So where is —" Flo started to ask.

She was interrupted by a gurgling moan from somewhere up above them. It echoed in the dark stairwell. A second later, they heard what sounded like a foot scraping against the sandy steps.

"It sounds like he's headed our way," Furry said, looking up. He pointed up the stairs. "Right there. See him?"

Flo squinted in the dim light of the stairwell. She could just barely make out a lumpy shape a few flights up. "Barely," she said. "I don't have wolf eyes like you, remember?"

"Oh," Furry said. "Right. I forgot. Well, he's coming."

Flo backed up until her foot hit the metal door. Furry stood his ground, waiting for the mummy to get closer.

"So . . . do we have a plan of some kind?" Flo asked. She couldn't believe Furry didn't seem more concerned. *For someone who's terrified of spiders, a rotting corpse in bandages sure doesn't seem to bother him*, she thought.

"Not really," Furry said. He shrugged his shoulders. "I guess we need to get him to the

crack and send him back where he belongs.
Same old, same old."

Furry let out a low whistle. "Jeez, he looks
a little unsteady," he said. "Maybe he should
hold on to the —"

As they watched, the mummy lurched and tipped forward, falling face-first down the steps. The monster landed in a pile on the landing, just inches away from where Flo and Furry stood.

"— handrail," Furry finished.

WRAP IT UP!

CHAPTER 3

Flo shuddered at her first glimpse of the mummy. She'd seen plenty of cartoon mummies in her time and even a fake one at the museum, but the real thing was even worse than she'd imagined.

Dingy, tattered strips of cloth were wrapped loosely around the mummy's head. The edges were frayed and loose, exposing the dark, shriveled skin of the monster beneath.

One of its eyes was half-open, and the other was missing completely. The monster's right leg seemed to be twisted in an odd angle, and a rib poked out through its chest wrappings.

"Is it dead?" Flo asked. "Still? Or . . . again, I guess?"

Furry got down on his hands and knees again and sniffed the fallen mummy. It was a little odd to see him act so much like a werewolf while he was still in human form.

"I'm not sure," Furry replied. "But we should probably get it out of here before it wakes up."

Flo took a step forward before she realized what Furry was asking her to do. "Hold up a second," she said. "There's no way I'm touching that thing. It looks like shriveled-up beef jerky."

"I can't do it alone," Furry said.

Flo took a deep breath and immediately wished she hadn't. She could actually *smell* the rotten mummy lying on the floor.

She was pretty tough, but touching a mummy from another world was asking too much. "Ugh, do I have to?" she asked.

"Just grab his legs and we can slide him," Furry said. He reached down and grabbed the mummy by the shoulders, digging his hands into the dingy wrappings.

Flo tried to hold her breath. The mummy stunk so badly.

"We'd better hurry up," Furry said. "I don't know how long it'll stay dead."

Flo wanted to refuse. But then she remembered how she'd felt when one of the Goblins Three had pulled Furry through the crack in the basement. She'd thought her friend was gone forever.

Who knows what'll happen if this thing wakes up and catches Furry, she thought. *I'd better just get it over with.*

"Fine," Flo muttered, grabbing the mummy's legs. "But my hands will never feel clean again."

Together Furry and Flo managed to slide the mummy down the stairs, bumping its lifeless head on each step on the way down. Flo figured out that if she breathed through her mouth the stink wasn't as bad.

As they neared the basement, the mummy started groaning. Suddenly, he raised an arm and swiped at Furry. Furry yelped and tried to jump back, but the creature caught hold of his necklace with a finger.

"Ah, its got me!" Furry cried. He pulled away, letting go of the mummy's bandage-wrapped shoulders.

Flo dropped the monster's feet, and they watched the miserable mummy tumble the rest of the way down the stairs. It came to a stop on the basement landing. With a final wheeze, the mummy fell lifeless again.

"It got my shard," Furry cried and touched his neck. He quickly leapt down the steps and crouched near the mummy.

"Your what?" Flo asked. She hurried after him, making sure to stay a safe distance from the pile of rags that was the mummy.

"Gimme that," Furry said. He pried the broken strap and blue shard from the mummy's lifeless hand. It didn't resist.

"What is that thing?" Flo asked.

"It's my shard," Furry said, looking relieved to have it back. "It's how I got to this world in the first place. I can't lose it."

Flo wanted to ask more about the shard, but glancing down at the mummy, she realized her questions would have to wait. *First we have to shove this stinky bag of bones back through the crack*, she thought.

Furry tried to put the necklace back around his neck, but the string had broken, and it was impossible.

"Here," Flo said. "Give it to me. I'll hold onto it for you." She opened her Dyno-Katz lunchbox and held it out to him.

Furry stared at it for a few moments. He seemed hesitant to let go of the necklace. Finally he took a deep breath and placed the necklace inside the lunchbox. "Keep it safe," he whispered.

"Don't worry," Flo said. "I never let this lunchbox out of my sight." She closed the top of the box and latched it. "It's as safe as it'll ever be."

Furry and Flo managed to drag the mummy out of the stairwell and down the hallway to the laundry room.

"Look at this," Flo said as they slid the mummy behind a bank of dryers and closer to the crack in the floor.

The piece of plywood that Curtis, Corman Towers' retired janitor, had placed over the crack was broken in half. It looked like something had punched its way through — hard. The blue crack glowed eerily underneath.

"Told you," Furry muttered, shaking his head. "The crack never stays sealed for long. There's always a way something can come through there."

Flo sighed. It was such a cruddy situation. She didn't want Furry to leave — he belonged here. But as long as he was in Flo's world, the crack stayed open. And she was getting a little tired of monsters slipping through.

"Let's get Ol' Stinky back where he belongs, then," Flo said. She set her lunchbox on the floor and held her breath as she squatted down next to the motionless mummy.

"On three?" Furry said, crouching down next to her. "We give him a shove and away he goes."

"Sure," Flo agreed. "Let's get this over with before someone else sees him."

"One," Furry said, putting his hands on the monster. "Two . . ."

Just then, the mummy groaned and lashed out. There was a metal clank as his twisted hand knocked against something.

"Three!" Furry hollered.

They gave him a hard shove, and the monster rolled toward the crack. Just like the goblins and the giant spider had been, the mummy was sucked though with a loud *WHOOSH!*

"Awesome," Furry cried. He stood up and brushed his hands on his shorts. "We're getting pretty good at this."

"No kidding," Flo agreed. She turned to pick up her lunchbox. But it was gone.

"No!" Flo screamed. She turned back and forth, scanning the floor for her beloved

Dyno-Katz lunchbox. But it was nowhere to be found.

"What?" Furry cried. "What's wrong?"

"It's gone! My lunchbox is gone," Flo said, gasping. "Oh, no, no, no!"

The news seemed to hit Furry like a punch to the stomach. He staggered back and put his hand against the gritty, cobweb-covered wall. "Oh, this is bad," he mumbled. "This is really, really bad."

"I have to get it back," Flo whispered, staring at the crack. "My dad gave that to me."

Before Furry could make a move to stop her, Flo stepped forward and put her foot at the edge of the blue crack. Just like the mummy, she was immediately sucked in.

WHOOSH!

PORTAL SHARD

CHAPTER 4

Flo had never been fired out of a giant circus cannon, but she imagined being sucked though the blue crack felt similar. One moment she was standing on solid concrete and the next she was hurtling through the air. She couldn't open her eyes, and it was hard to breathe.

Suddenly, Flo felt herself falling. Hot air rushed past her face, and she slammed into something soft, but gritty feeling. She didn't have to look to know she'd somehow landed in sand.

Flo finally opened her eyes and squinted at the shimmering expanse of desert before her. It seemed to stretch forever. "Holy socks," she said, gasping.

In the distance were the hugest sand dunes Flo had ever seen. There were at least ten of them spread across the horizon. They rose up toward the sky, seeming to almost touch the clouds.

It took Flo a moment to realize that what she was seeing wasn't sand dunes at all — they were giant pyramids. All around them, grand temples and beautiful statues decorated the landscape.

It looks like some sort of ancient city, Flo thought.

Flo stood up and felt the sand sift from her clothing. She brushed it off her arms and legs and used her hand to shield her eyes from the sun. "Where am I?" she wondered aloud.

As Flo stared at the horizon, something howled and landed behind her with a loud *THUMP!*

Flo turned around to see Furry, in his
werewolf form, lying on his back in the sand.
The scorching sand must have been even
hotter for someone wearing a full-body fur
coat, because the little werewolf quickly leapt

up onto his paws and shook the gritty sand from his fur.

"Dang, this sand gets everywhere," Furry muttered. His tongue hung out of his mouth, and he panted in the scorching heat. "And it's hot here."

"Yeah . . . about that. Where is *here* exactly?" Flo asked.

"My world," Furry said, glancing around. "My old one, I mean. And coming here was *not* one of your better ideas."

Flo looked back toward the desert city and the enormous pyramids. "No one asked you to follow me," she said.

"Well, I couldn't just leave you here all alone," Furry said. "What kind of friend would I be if I did that? Besides, my shard is in your lunchbox, remember? I have to get it back."

"Why is that necklace so important to you, anyway?" Flo asked. "I don't get it."

"It's not just a necklace," Furry explained. "It's a portal shard. It's how I ended up in your world in the first place."

"So it's like a key of some kind?" Flo asked.

"Sort of," Furry said. "I was playing around one day, and I made a crack in the seal that leads from my world to yours. That's how I came through."

Flo looked around the sandy landscape. "So where's the crack now?" she asked. "I don't see anything."

"There isn't one," Furry said. "The shard was what was keeping it open. As soon as it went back through, the crack started to seal itself back up. I barely made it through before it closed."

"I thought *you* being in our world was keeping the crack open," Flo said. "Isn't that why all those monsters have been coming through and trashing our apartment building? And how are we supposed to get back if there's no crack?"

"I think some of them *are* coming through to get me," Furry said. "But it was the shard that was keeping the portal open."

Furry turned away from Flo and started digging. In moments, he'd uncovered a small stone circle embedded in the sand. The edges were worn, but a decorative pattern ran around the edge.

"This is our way home," Furry said. "But we have to get the shard back. That's the only way to reopen the seal. And we only have until sunset."

Flo crossed her arms. "What happens at sunset?" she asked.

"The portal changes," Furry explained. "Not all the paths lead to the same place. Who knows where we'll end up. But it sure won't be Corman Towers."

"How do you know?" Flo asked.

Furry grinned at her. "You're in my world now, remember?" he said. He looked around the sandy desert again, seeming a little confused. "Even if I don't really recognize this part of it."

Flo checked the horizon for any sign of the mummy, but she didn't see it anywhere. She couldn't even see any footprints that would let them follow its trail. The mummy seemed to have completely disappeared — with her lunchbox.

"Well, I guess we both have something we need to find, then," Flo said. "What happens if we don't get the shard back?"

"Then we're stuck here forever," Furry whispered.

AFTER THAT MUMMY!

CHAPTER 5

Furry and Flo started walking toward the city in the sand. Flo thought it would take forever to reach the city. And when the wind started blowing sand in their faces, it felt even longer.

I could really go for some air-conditioning, Flo thought as she wiped sweat off her forehead.

After they'd been walking for several minutes, Flo glanced back behind them.

The wind had blown sand into their tracks, making it impossible to see where they'd started.

"Um . . . you remember how to get back to the portal, right?" she asked Furry. "Like, where it is?"

"Don't worry," Furry said. He was panting. His doggy tongue hung out of his mouth. "I might not know exactly where we are, but I'll find it. What do you think this nose of mine is good for?"

"How do you not know where we are?" Flo said. "I thought this was *your* world."

50

"It is," Furry said. "But it's just as big as yours. Maybe even bigger. I mean, think about it. Have you been every single place in *your* world?"

"Good point," Flo admitted. She watched her werewolf friend blink as sand blasted across his eyes and stuck in his fur. He was covered head to paw in grit. The poor little beast looked miserable.

"Why don't you switch back to being a person?" Flo suggested. She noticed Furry still had his swimming trunks on. They'd obviously been through a few werewolf transformations. Flo could see that they'd been sewn back together in a few places. "You'd probably be a lot cooler."

Furry flashed her an extra-toothy wolf grin. "Nothing is cooler than a werewolf," he said. "Besides, I can't. In my world, I'm always a werewolf."

"Even if you burp?" Flo asked. She'd learned a few weeks ago that when Furry wanted to change back into his human form, all he needed to do was burp. It was gross, but effective.

Furry shook his head. "That trick doesn't work here," he said. "I was never a human until I showed up in your world and Curtis found me. I just have to stay like this. If we get back, I'll change."

Flo shot him a look.

"*When* we get back, I mean," Furry said. "We will."

Flo turned away and kept walking. *This crazy sand world has our stuff*, she thought. *We're not leaving without it.*

* * *

Flo wasn't sure how long it took them
to reach the city, but by the time they got
close, she was ready to collapse. "So, how are
we going to find this missing mummy?" she
asked. "Do you think someone sent it through
to find you?"

Furry shook his head. "I doubt it. Like I
said, mummies aren't the smartest monsters.
It probably fell through the crack on this side
by accident."

Up ahead was a large stone platform. Flo
stepped onto it and spotted two tall figures.
They wore ornate, golden armor that shone in
the desert sun. Their skin was painted a deep,
dark black, and they wore large animal masks
on their heads. One had the head of a hawk
and the other the head of a dog.

As Flo watched, the figures poked a bunch of balled-up rags on the ground.

"Back into the sand, wretch!" the hawk-headed soldier said. "You are not permitted passage inside!"

Suddenly Flo realized the soldiers weren't simply looking at trash in the sand. "It's the mummy!" she whispered.

The soldiers gave the mummy another hard shove, and the pile of rags toppled over the edge. It landed face down in the hot, gritty sand.

As Flo raced across the stone platform, the mummy buried itself deeper into the desert. By the time she reached the edge, it had disappeared.

"No!" Flo shouted, forgetting about the animal-headed guards. It was only when Furry growled and scampered closer that she realized her mistake.

"Flo," Furry barked. "We've got a problem here!"

Flo had never seen Furry look so angry. His big teeth showed as he growled at the tall soldiers. He looked ready to attack if either of them made a move.

"You will come with us, beast," the hawk-headed soldier commanded. "You and the stranger."

"Look, we don't want any trouble," Flo said. When she spoke, the dog-headed soldier turned to face her. She couldn't tell if the creature was angry or not, so she keep talking. "We just want our stuff back. That mummy stole —"

"Silence, stranger," the dog-headed guard interrupted. He didn't shout or seem angry. His voice was flat and direct.

"Okay, okay," Flo said. She put her hands up. After all, that's what people did on TV when they needed to surrender.

"We need to run, Flo," Furry growled through his teeth. "I don't want to get stuck here."

"Well, we're not going anywhere without our stuff," Flo whispered back. She took a step forward and squinted as the sun glinted off the soldiers' armor. "We give up."

THE PALACE OF BASTET

CHAPTER 6

Flo knew Furry wasn't happy about surrendering, but she didn't know what else to do. There was no way they could take on the giant animal-headed soldiers and expect to win. The hawk-headed one held Furry by the scruff of his neck, making him whimper as he trotted to keep up. The dog-headed one gripped the back of Flo's T-shirt, making sure she stayed with them.

The soldiers led them deeper into the city. They climbed ornately carved stone steps, walked beneath grand archways, and passed giant statues of other animal-headed creatures. The sitting sculptures stared out into the desert, their hands resting patiently on their enormous laps.

"This is just like ancient Egypt," Flo whispered to Furry.

It was true. Flo had seen enough at the museum to recognize the towering pyramids, giant statues, and hieroglyphics that covered almost every surface. It was like they'd traveled back in time, before centuries of sandstorms had buried ancient Egyptian civilizations.

And yet, there was still something that seemed off.

As they continued through the city streets, Flo realized that none of the "people" she'd seen looked human. Everyone was incredibly tall and had dark mud smeared over any exposed skin. They all wore masks with large, oval-shaped eyes that had curly swirls at the ends. As Furry and Flo passed, the crowd stared from behind their unblinking masks.

"I don't think being captured is going to help us get our stuff back," Furry said. He yelped as the guard pinched his fur again. "That mummy had it."

Flo didn't know what to say, so she kept quiet. It didn't make her feel any better to see the sun sinking lower in the sky. *If we don't get back to that portal before the sun goes down*, she thought, *we're going to be stuck here forever.*

They continued through the city until they reached a golden palace. Jewel-covered pillars flanked the grand entrance. The soldiers stopped Furry and Flo, pausing in front of a pair of enormous doors.

"Now we're getting somewhere," Flo whispered to Furry. "Someone important must live here. Maybe they'll help us find my lunchbox."

"Do you recognize anything?" Flo asked, looking around.

Furry shook his head. "We must be a long way from where I grew up," he whispered.

Somewhere inside the palace, a horn sounded. A moment later, the magnificently carved doors opened outward. Two more animal-headed soldiers, both wearing lion-head masks, stood inside.

"This is the palace of Bastet," the hawk-headed soldier announced. "Here, your fates will be decided."

Flo cringed. *That really doesn't sound good*, she thought.

"I don't like the sound of that," Furry growled under his breath. "We should've run when we had the chance."

"Silence, beast!" the dog-headed soldier ordered.

The guards pushed Furry and Flo into the palace and led them down a shadowy hallway. Statues and paintings of cat-like creatures adorned the walls. In the paintings, other animal-headed beings seemed to be offering gifts to the cats.

What is this place? Flo wondered as she glanced around. She knew she couldn't get too wrapped up in the strange world. Their visit needed to be short if they hoped to get back to the portal in time.

If we can find it again, that is, Flo thought.

The animal-headed guards pushed them through a tall archway, and Flo found herself standing in a grand throne room. A tall cat-like creature wearing a long white gown and an elegant black mask sat atop a jewel-encrusted throne.

The soldiers both knelt before the creature. "Behold," they said in unison. "The goddess Bastet."

Flo looked at Furry. "Are we supposed to bow or something?" she asked.

Furry shrugged. "How should I know?"

"What else has this day brought before me?" the goddess asked.

"We found these two near the farthest desert view," the dog-headed guard replied. "They hoped to steal our treasures."

Flo glared at him but kept her mouth shut. *Treasures?* she thought furiously. *We just wanted what was taken from us!*

Bastet shifted on her throne. Like the soldiers, her exposed skin was painted a

deep, dark black. Small sapphire circles were wrapped around her arms and wrists. In one hand she held a tall, golden scepter. Like everything else in the sand city, the scepter looked like it had come straight from a book on ancient Egypt.

Then Flo saw something that interested her way more than the throne room's splendor. Clutched in Bastet's left hand was Flo's Dyno-Katz lunchbox.

THE
CAT BOX

CHAPTER 7

Flo took a step toward Bastet's throne. "That's m—" she started to say. But the dog-headed soldier immediately stopped her.

"These creatures are curious to me," Bastet said, rising from her throne. Flo's lunchbox dangled from her ring-covered fingers. "They are not like us."

You got that right, cat lady, Flo thought. She wanted nothing more than to snatch her lunchbox and make a break for it. But there were guards everywhere. They wouldn't get far. *Well, maybe Furry would*, Flo realized, *but not me.*

"What is to be their fate, my goddess?" the hawk-headed guard asked, bowing his head. "Their arrival could bring impending doom to our people."

Bastet stepped down from her raised throne and studied Furry and Flo. "Throw them into the pits," she said with a wave of her ringed hand.

Instantly, the guards grabbed Flo and Furry and began dragging them out of Bastet's chamber. Flo had no idea what the pits were, but they sounded like . . . well, the pits.

"Wait!" Flo shouted frantically. "I know about that box you found! I'll tell you all about it!"

The servants and guards all gasped and
froze in fear. Everyone stared at the cat-
headed goddess, waiting for her reaction.

Bastet gazed at Flo through her black
mask. "How dare you speak out of turn?!" she
said. "And what do you know of this treasure?
My servants found it in my kingdom!"

Flo didn't care if she angered the cat goddess. She wasn't leaving without her lunchbox. "That mummy took it from me!" Flo cried. "It came from my world and I need to get it back."

"But why?" Bastet said. "It has images of cats upon it. Surely the gods meant for me to have it."

Flo smiled as an idea began to form. She knew she only had one chance, though. Otherwise, they were headed for the pits.

"The cat box is dangerous," Flo warned. "It contains something that can crack your world in two. I've come to take it back so you and your people can live in peace."

Bastet raised the lunchbox up to examine it. She turned it in her hands and Flo heard the contents clank around inside.

"It is unlike anything I've ever seen," Bastet marveled. "I do not know the story of the cats upon it. Are they the bringers of destruction?"

Flo nodded. "I'll tell you their tale," she said softly. "If you'll let me."

Bastet nodded to the dog-headed guard, who immediately released Flo.

"Will you let my dog go, too?" Flo asked.

"Hey!" Furry protested. "I'm not your —"

"We mean you no harm," Flo said, interrupting her friend.

Bastet waved her free hand toward the other guard, who quickly released Furry as well. Bastet motioned for Flo to come closer.

Flo stepped up near the throne and pointed at the lunchbox. "All of these cats are fighters," she said. She pointed to the green cat on the front. It held three sticks of

dynamite taped together. "This is Blast Kat. She can topple mountains with her bombs."

"Bombs?" Bastet repeated, sounding confused.

Furry looked confused too, and Flo realized she'd never told him the full story behind her most-treasured possession.

"Magic sticks that can destroy things," Flo explained. Next she pointed to the red cat wearing an eye patch and holding a sword. "This is Kutty Kat. Her blade can slice through any armor or metal. This one episode —"

"You speak in riddles, tiny stranger," the goddess interrupted.

"Sorry," Flo said. She'd gotten carried away. "Let's just say that even giants fall when she swings her sword."

Bastet was silent for a moment. "And the last one?" she finally asked.

"That's Acro Kat," Flo said. "She's fast, sneaky, and deadly. No creature alive can catch up with her. She could be anywhere, hiding in the shadows, waiting."

"What does the Acro Kat wait for?" Bastet asked.

Flo smiled. She knew she had the goddess's interest now. "Like any good cat stalking its prey, she waits for the perfect moment to *STRIKE!*"

As she spoke, Flo leapt into action. She grabbed the lunchbox, wrenched it free from Bastet's hands, and tossed it in Furry's direction. "Furry, catch!"

The goddess gasped as the lunchbox sailed across the throne room. Furry bounded across the shiny floor. His paws slipped, but he recovered and leapt into the air, catching the lunchbox handle in his teeth. He immediately turned tail and ran toward the hallway.

"Seize them!" Bastet shrieked. "And bring the cat box to me!"

Flo jumped down from the elevated throne and quickly raced after Furry. They had to escape . . . *now!*

RUN, FURRY, RUN!

CHAPTER 8

Flo raced after Furry, hoping the little werewolf knew where he was going. Guards ran after them shouting angrily, and sandaled feet pounded on the floor. Somewhere in the palace, a horn sounded. It felt like everyone in the sand city was after them.

"Seal the palace!" a voice shouted. Flo looked up and saw that the entrance they'd come through was quickly being closed.

Apparently their way *in* wasn't going to be their way *out*.

Furry stood up on his hind legs and grabbed the lunchbox with a free paw. "We have to find another way out!" he barked. "C'mon!"

Flo ran as fast as she could, but she was still no match for a werewolf. "I'm not as fast as you!" she hollered.

"Aw, that's right," Furry groaned. He doubled back and snatched Flo up, carrying her in his furry arms like a football.

"Don't drop me," Flo begged.

"Don't worry, I won't," Furry promised as he darted up a set of stairs.

Flo noticed her hairy friend was panting again. "And try not to slobber on me, either," she said.

"That I can't promise," Furry said. He plunked the lunchbox into Flo's hands. "Hold that, okay?"

Flo clutched her lunchbox tightly as Furry picked up speed. Ornate statues and wall hangings went by in a blur as he raced down another hallway. He darted between startled guards, whipped around a corner, and blasted through a wooden door. They finally came to a halt in a large room.

"I think we'll be safe here for a few minutes," Furry said, setting Flo on her feet. He closed the door behind him and started dragging a huge statue of Bastet across the room.

"Isn't that thing heavy?" Flo asked. She couldn't believe how easy the little werewolf made it look.

Furry shrugged as he moved the statue easily. "I guess," he said. "But that's where my werewolf strength comes in handy. Too bad this fur is so stinking hot."

Once the door was blocked, Flo relaxed a moment. *At least we're safe for a couple minutes*, she thought. *But we still need to find another way out.*

Suddenly Furry's nose perked up, and he sniffed the air curiously. "Do you smell that?" he asked.

Flo took a deep breath, and for the second time that day, immediately wished that she hadn't. It smelled like an animal had had an accident somewhere. She turned around and noticed a large stone square on the floor at the other end of the room. It appeared to be filled with dark sand.

A small servant stood at one end of the sand pool. He wore a mask that resembled a lion's head, but the face was more human than the others. A rectangular stone beard hung from his chin.

The servant picked up a rake and began raking clumps of something from the sand. "What brings you to this place?" he asked. Unlike everyone else they'd met, he didn't sound angry or scared to find two strangers in the palace.

"We're trying to get out of here," Furry said. "This place stinks."

Hearing the word *stinks* jogged Flo's memory, and she suddenly realized why the servant's face looked familiar. She'd seen it in the ancient Egypt exhibit at the museum back home.

"You're the Sphinx!" Flo exclaimed with a gasp.

"How do you know my name?" Sphinx asked, sounding surprised.

"There's a giant statue of you where I come from," Flo said. "My world has all sorts of stuff from this place!"

Furry covered his nose with a paw. He looked at the Sphinx with his rake and seemed to realize what the servant's job was. "Are you raking kitty litter?" he asked.

Sphinx looked down at the sand pool before him. "My job is to clean the goddess's fragrant sand."

"Yeah . . . we call that a litter box back home," Flo said.

"Alas," Sphinx said, sighing. "It is not a fitting task for someone of my wisdom."

Suddenly Flo remembered something else from her trip to the museum. "Aren't you good at riddles?" she asked.

Sphinx nodded. "It's one of my gifts."

Just then, something big and heavy struck the door. It sounded like the guards were trying to batter down the door.

"Uh, Flo?" Furry said, looking around. "We should probably go."

Flo scanned the room, trying to find a different way out. There was the door they'd come in, but with the guards waiting on the other side, it was hardly an option at all. Other than that, there was only one window.

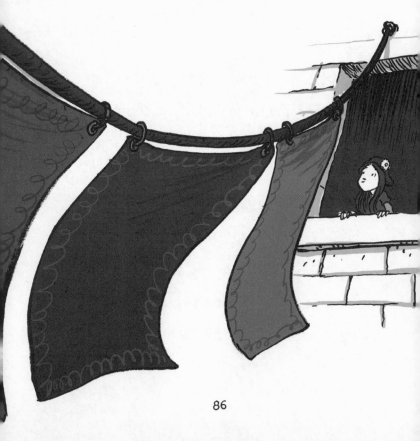

Flo ran to the window and stuck her head out. A rope with large tapestries ran from the palace to a shorter building across the courtyard. It whipped back and forth in the desert wind. Flo glanced down. It was way too far for them to jump. Even worse, the sun had sunk far lower in the sky, casting an orange glow on the rest of the sand city.

"I think we're trapped," Flo said.

NO TIME FOR RIDDLES

CHAPTER 9

The door rattled again as the guards tried to get in. With every strike, it seemed to weaken. Not even the heavy statue Furry had dragged in front of it would slow them for long.

"Why are they after you?" Sphinx asked, leaning on his rake. He didn't seem bothered by the giant guards slamming against the door.

"Because we took this back from Bastet!" Flo said, holding her lunchbox up. "Bastet thinks it's some kind of treasure. And it is, but only to me. Now her soldiers are coming to get us."

"And throw us in the pits," Furry added. He was back down on all fours and ran around in circles like a dog that needed to be let outside. "Whatever that is."

Sphinx nodded. "That is unfortunate," he said. "Well, I must finish raking the fragrant sands if I'm to get my day's meal. It is miserable work, but I do as the goddess bids. We all must."

Sphinx went back to dragging his rake through the sand, kicking up a stink.

Just then, Flo remembered the turkey sandwich in her lunchbox. She never left home without one. "If you help us out, I'll give you a meal right now," she offered.

"I have a better idea," Sphinx said. "I'll speak a riddle to you. If you can tell me the answer, I'll give you my rake."

Furry stopped. "What good is a rake going to do us?" he snapped. "We just need to get back home."

Just then, the door rattled again loudly.

"It's better than nothing," Flo said. "We'll take it. Hit us with your best riddle. And make it fast."

Sphinx set the rake down and clapped his hands excitedly. "What can be seen everywhere, makes up our land, yet slips between the fingers of your hand?" Sphinx asked. He crossed his arms, awaiting their answer.

Seen everywhere, but slips between the fingers of your hand? Flo thought, pacing the floor. She tried to concentrate, but it was hard with the guards determined to bang down the door.

Flo looked around the room. *What can I see everywhere? Cats?* She saw them everywhere, at least in the palace, but it didn't sound right.

BOOM! The door splintered, and an animal-headed guard peered through the jagged hole. There was no time left!

Flo unlatched her lunchbox and pulled out one of her famous

turkey sandwiches. "Are you sure you don't just want a sand—"

"You've guessed it!" Sphinx shouted, interrupting her.

"I did?" Flo asked, trying to figure out exactly what she'd said. Then it hit her — sand! She meant to say "sandwich," but it was good enough for Sphinx. "I mean, yes. Sand is the answer!"

"Perfect!" Furry shouted. "So you'll help us?"

"You've won my rake," Sphinx announced. He tossed the rake to Flo.

"Oh," Furry said. "Perfect."

The wind outside kicked up, whipping the tapestries back and forth against the room's open window. Suddenly Flo had an idea. She picked up the rake, tossed the sandwich to

Sphinx, and ran to the window. *This could work*, she thought.

"Furry!" she shouted, "get over here!"

The werewolf ran to the window. "What's the plan?" he asked.

"We're going to make a zip line," Flo said. "If we hook the rake over the top of the rope, we can zip across to the other building. We'll be closer to the ground, and then we can make a run for it."

Furry grabbed the rake and stepped into the window's opening. With a grunt, he hooked the end of the rake over the rope and held on with both paws.

Just then the door exploded open behind them. The Bastet statue toppled over and hit the stone floor, shattering into a thousand pieces.

"Let's go!" Flo cried. As the guards raced to grab them, she wrapped her arms around Furry and they leapt out the window.

The ride along the rope was quick and more than a little scary. Flo clutched her lunchbox tightly as they soared across the stone courtyard. The wind kicked up again, catching the tapestries they zipped past. The heavy fabric bunched up ahead of them as they slid.

I hope Furry has a good grip on that rake, Flo thought nervously.

In seconds, they were approaching the wall of the shorter structure.

"Hang on tight," Furry said. "I'm going to let go. Then we'd better run like our lives depend on it."

"Um . . . they kind of do," Flo said.

Furry let go of the rake and they dropped to the ground. Furry landed solidly on his feet and caught Flo in his arms. Before the rake could clatter to the ground, they were off, racing toward the desert.

From the palace window above, Flo heard Sphinx shout. "This sand itch . . . it's delicious!"

INTO THE
DESERT

CHAPTER 10

"Whatever you do, don't let go of that lunchbox," Furry warned her as they ran. "That portal shard is the only way out of here!"

Flo gulped. She definitely didn't want to be trapped in Furry's world forever. They raced through the walkways of the city, avoiding any guards they spotted. They snuck behind walls and ducked into shadowy corners created by the rapidly setting sun.

They finally reached the stone platform at the edge of the desert. Furry glanced up at the looming pyramids. "We have to hurry if we're going to make it back to the portal before the sun sets."

Behind them, they heard the roar of the guards. Flo turned to see a swarm of animal-headed soldiers headed their way.

"Let's go," Furry cried. "They're coming!"

Flo raced after Furry into the desert. The werewolf was down on all fours, sniffing the ground. She hoped he'd be able to pick up their scent and lead them back to the portal again — fast.

As they ran, the winds started to pick up, throwing more sand across the sky than ever before. Flo's hair whipped across her face so much that she could barely see a thing.

Just then, Furry stopped. "Something isn't right," he said. He backed up a few feet, and Flo nearly ran into him before she stopped too.

The sun dipped lower on the horizon. In minutes, they'd be in complete darkness, and their way home would disappear.

"What?" Flo asked, glancing back over her shoulder nervously. She expected the guards to be right behind them.

But the animal-headed soldiers were no longer chasing after them. They'd stopped at the edge of the desert and were watching from a distance.

It's almost like they're scared to come out here, Flo thought. *But why?*

Suddenly a rag-covered hand reached up from the sand and swiped at Flo's ankle. A

moment later, another one emerged. Then another and another. A few feet away, an entire head popped up. The swatches of cloth around the face clued Furry and Flo in.

"You have to be kidding me," Flo shouted. "The desert is filled with mummies!"

"Yep," Furry cried. "They're all over the desert. No wonder one fell through the crack!"

Everywhere they turned, more and more mummies were pulling themselves out of the sand. Flo suddenly understood why the guards stayed back on the stone platform.

"They're not going to want us to leave again," Furry warned. "Especially if it means taking the shard with us. Run!"

As the twisted hands and rotten mouths swiped at them, Flo and Furry raced through the sandstorm. The sky grew darker with every step they took. The mummies groaned and lumbered clumsily after them.

Flo opened her mouth to shout, but it was quickly coated with sand. "Ugh," she grumbled, spitting sand. "Are we close?"

"Yeah," Furry shouted. He growled at a mummy who grabbed one of his legs. "It should be right here!"

They both stopped to look around. The stone circle they'd come through was gone. Flo panicked. Not only had the way home disappeared, but hundreds of stinky, rotten mummies were headed their way. As if to prove her point, a hand shot up through the sand near her foot.

"Let's start digging," Furry cried.

"Are you nuts?" Flo said. "We might dig up more mummies!"

"We don't have a choice!" Furry yelled. "Either we find the portal or we're stuck here!"

Furry immediately started pawing through the sand. Sand shot past either side of him, rivaling the growing sand storm in the desert.

Since Furry could dig so much faster, Flo focused on keeping the approaching mummies away. More and more of the creepy beings had caught up to them, and even more were emerging from the sand. In moments, they'd be surrounded.

In the dark, she thought. *With no way home. With mummies closing in on us.*

The last sliver of sunlight was burning above a far-off sand dune when Furry let out a happy bark. "Found it!" he yelled, frantically clearing the sand away from the circular stone. "Quick, hand me the shard!"

Flo smacked a mummy with her lunchbox, knocking the tattered monster back a step

or two. She shook another one off her ankle and opened the lunchbox. It was almost completely dark, and she could only hope everything else inside wouldn't tumble out.

With quick fingers, she found the blue shard. "Here!" she cried. She slapped it into Furry's outstretched paw and quickly snapped her Dyno-Katz lunchbox shut again.

Furry held the shard between his fingers
and scratched a thin line across the width of
the stone circle.

Nothing happened.

"Uh-oh," Furry said. "I thought it —"

There was a sudden flash of light and
the seal glowed, opening into a familiar blue
portal. The mummies staggered backward,
and Furry and Flo dove through the crack.

THROUGH THE
CRACK

CHAPTER 11

Flo's stomach churned, and in a flash, she felt something cold against her face. She heard water sloshing in the background, and for a second she worried they'd ended up somewhere else. But with one deep whiff of fabric softener, Flo knew.

We're home, she thought gratefully.

Furry sat up next to her, still in his werewolf state, and groaned. "Oh, my head hurts," he mumbled.

"Is someone back there?" a woman's voice called. "Hello?"

Flo's eyes widened. "It's my mom," she whispered.

The footsteps came closer, and Flo quickly popped open her lunchbox and tossed a juice box to Furry. The little werewolf ignored the straw, popping the entire juice box into his mouth. His sharp teeth sliced the juice container to pieces, and Furry let out a loud *BURP!* He immediately changed back into his human form.

"Flo?" her mom called, raising her voice. "Is that you?" A moment later, she poked her head over the top of a dryer. "What in the world are you two doing back here? I've been looking everywhere for you! You're both filthy. And full of sand . . . again."

"Oh, you know, just got back from the desert," Flo joked, quickly getting to her feet. Furry hopped up too and they stood side by side to hide the dimly glowing blue crack from view.

Flo's mom just sighed and shook her head at them. "You two and your imaginations," she said.

"Yeah," Furry said. "Deserts are pretty sandy."

"Well, go out front and dump the desert outside, would you?" Flo's mom said. "Then come upstairs to eat your cold dinner, Flo. Maybe when school starts next week you two will stay out of trouble."

Doubtful, Flo thought. But she breathed a sigh of relief all the same.

* * *

On the sidewalk in front of Corman Towers, Flo pulled off her shoes and dumped the sand into some nearby bushes. "I never want to see sand again," she grumbled. She shook her shoe one last time for good measure.

Furry stood in his tattered swim shorts and pulled his pockets inside out. A bit of

sand sifted out onto the pavement. "Me neither," he admitted.

Flo knew she needed to get back upstairs, but she sat down for a moment. Furry plopped down next to her, and they stared for a few minutes at the traffic honking its way past their building.

Eventually Flo spoke up. "I don't get why we can't just toss the shard into the crack and be done with it," she said. "I mean, if that's what's keeping the crack open, we'd be safer without it, right? No more crack, no more monsters. Problem solved."

Furry was quiet as he stared at the park. "It's not that easy," he finally said. "If I ever want to go back home, I have to hold on to it."

"Go back home?" Flo repeated. "You mean you'd really leave? For good?" She couldn't imagine Corman Towers without her best friend.

Furry shrugged. "I get homesick sometimes," he admitted. "And my parents must miss me. I mean, they sent the goblins after me, right?"

Flo nodded. "Sure seems like it," she said.

"I know me being here is dangerous, but I like it here," Furry said. He gave Flo a small smile. "Especially now that I have a friend like you. It's hard to think about leaving, but it's hard to think about not being able to. It's just hard to let go."

Flo was quiet for a moment. "Yeah, I know what you mean," she said. "I'm going to show you something."

She took a deep breath and opened the lunchbox. Inside were an uneaten sandwich, another juice box, and a small photo. Flo picked up the photo carefully and held it out to Furry. "Look at this," she said.

Furry looked at the picture and frowned. "It's some guy at a drawing table with a little kid sitting on his lap. So?"

Flo smiled. "That kid is me," she said. "And that's my dad."

"Oh," Furry said quietly.

"He's not around anymore," Flo said. "But when he was, things were different. Dad was an artist. He used to draw cartoons."

That got Furry's attention. "Really?" he asked, perking up. "Which ones? I love cartoons. It's one of my favorite things about this world."

Flo sighed. "My dad created Dyno-Katz," she said.

Furry scratched his head and looked at the picture again. "Weird," he said. "I've never heard of Dyno-Katz. Was it on TV?"

Flo shook her head. "It never made it to TV," she said. "It was my dad's dream, though. He worked so hard on it. One of the networks decided they wanted a whole season of episodes."

"So what happened?" Furry asked. "How come it was never on TV?"

"It fell apart," Flo said. She turned the picture over so she could look at it, too. "They decided not to do the show."

Furry sat quietly. Flo put the picture safely back in her lunchbox and closed the lid carefully.

"They were going to make Dyno-Katz toys, games, breakfast cereal, you name it. One of the companies made this lunchbox as a test," Flo explained. "My dad was so excited. But a few days later, they changed their minds. The company never made another one. That's why the lunchbox is really special to me. So, I understand. It's hard to let go."

Furry nodded. "I get it now," he said. "It's one of a kind. Just like you, Flo."

"Oh, stop it," Flo said. "That just sounds corny."

Furry laughed. "Corny, but true," he said with a grin.

Flo stood and looked up at the looming, beat-up building. "I have to get back," she said. "My mom is probably wondering what's taking so long."

"Yeah, okay," Furry replied. "I'm glad you got your lunchbox back."

Flo smiled. "Thanks," she said. "I'm glad you got your shard back. Thanks for coming in after me."

Furry stood up too. "Hey," he said. "What're friends for?"

Lots of things, Flo thought as they walked inside. *But best friends are something else entirely — even if they drool sometimes.*

THE AUTHOR

Thomas Kingsley Troupe writes, makes movies, and works as a firefighter/EMT. He's written many books for kids, including *Legend of the Vampire* and *Mountain Bike Hero*, and has two boys of his own. He likes zombies, bacon, orange Popsicles, and reading stories to his kids. Thomas currently lives in Woodbury, Minnesota, with his super cool family.

THE ILLUSTRATOR

Stephen Gilpin is the illustrator of several dozen children's books and is currently working on a project he hopes will give him the ability to walk through walls — although he acknowledges there is still a lot of work to be done on this project. He currently lives in Hiawatha, Kansas, with his genius wife, Angie, and their kids.

THE SKELETONS IN CITY PARK

The rest of Flo's morning passed by smoothly. Everything seemed to be going well until they started the math unit. Her teacher, Mrs. Shamp, had just handed out their workbooks for reviewing fractions when Flo saw something thin and white sneaking past the ground-floor window.

"What was that?" Flo blurted out before she could stop herself.

"Flo?" Mrs. Shamp asked. "Is everything okay?"

Flo looked away from the window and realized everyone was staring at her. *Great*, she thought. *Not only am I the new kid, but I'm the weird new kid.*

"Um, yeah," Flo said quickly. "I just thought I saw something outside."

"Well, if you see it again, let me know," Mrs. Shamp said. "Now you've got me curious."

A few of the kids in the class laughed.

Flo took a deep breath and let it out slowly. She tried to force herself to focus on the instructions for completing the worksheet correctly. But she couldn't help it. She glanced back up at the window.

Flo gasped. There it was again — a skeleton.

CATCH UP
ON ALL OF
FURRY
AND FLO'S
ADVENTURES